W9-CNG-190

**DO NOT REMOVE
CARDS FROM POCKET**

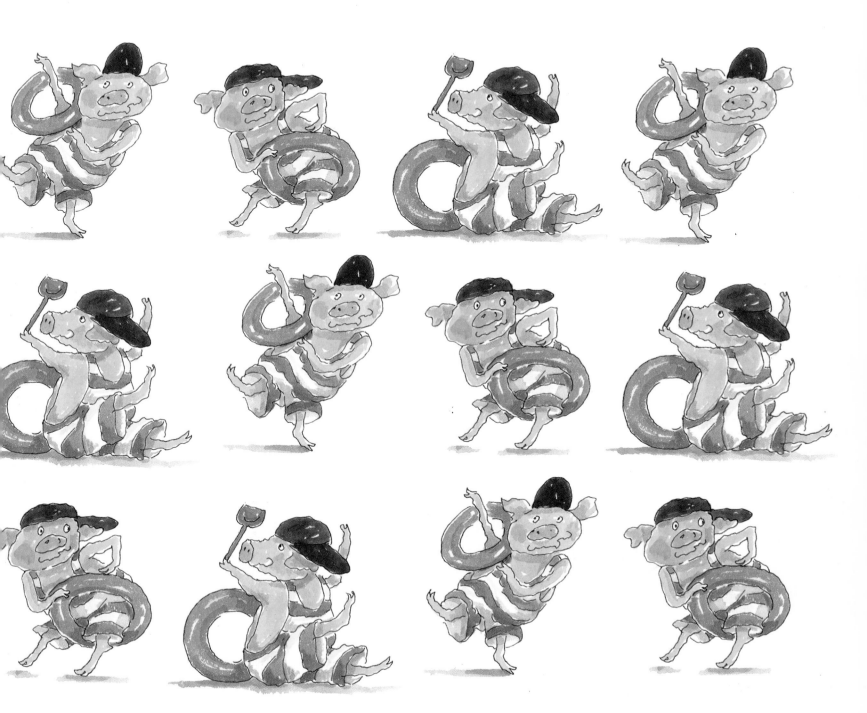

For Matthew, with love

S.J.P.

Text copyright © 1991 by Jon Blake
Illustrations copyright © 1991 by Susie Jenkin-Pearce
First published in Great Britain in 1991 by Hutchinson Children's Books.
All rights reserved. No part of this book may be reproduced
or utilized in any form or by any means, electronic or
mechanical, including photocopying, recording, or by any
information storage or retrieval system, without
permission in writing from the Publisher.
Inquiries should be addressed to Tambourine Books,
a division of William Morrow & Company, Inc.,
1350 Avenue of the Americas, New York, New York 10019.
Printed and bound in Belgium by Proost International Book Production

Library of Congress Cataloging-in-Publication Data
Blake, Jon.   Wriggly Pig/Jon Blake;
pictures by Susie Jenkin-Pearce.— 1st U.S. ed.   p.   cm.
Summary: Wriggly Pig drives his family crazy with his wiggling
and fidgeting, until a near disaster shows them that they
prefer him moving to still.
ISBN 0-688-11295-1 (trade) — ISBN 0-688-11296-X (lib.)
[1. Pigs—Fiction.   2. Behavior—Fiction.]
I. Jenkin-Pearce. Susie, ill.   II. Title.
PZ7.B554Wr   1992   [E]—dc20   91-24171   CIP   AC

1   3   5   7   9   10   8   6   4   2
First U.S. edition, 1992

Jon Blake

WRIGGLY PIG

illustrated by Susie Jenkin-Pearce

Tambourine Books  New York

The Pigs were getting ready for their afternoon out. Mr. Walter Pig was ready.

Mrs. Betty Pig was ready.

Bradley Pig was ready and Brenda Pig was ready. But Wriggly Pig was not ready.

"Keep still, Wriggly Pig!" said Mr. Pig, as he buttoned Wriggly's jacket.

But Wriggly Pig would not keep still.

"He should have been a worm," said Mrs. Pig.

The Pigs went for a ride in the car. Bradley sat straight and looked out of the left window. Brenda sat even straighter and looked out of the right window. But Wriggly Pig fidgeted and squirmed and tried to look out of all the windows at once.

"Keep still, Wriggly Pig!" said Mrs. Pig. "I can't see the cars behind us!" But Wriggly Pig would not keep still.

"He's got ants in his pants," said Mr. Pig.

The Pigs arrived at the movies.
Soon Mr. and Mrs. Pig and
Brenda and Bradley were glued
to the screen.

But Wriggly Pig was not
glued to anything. He shuffled
and shifted and rustled his
popcorn.

"Keep still, Wriggly Pig!"
said the goats behind. "We can't
see the picture!"

But Wriggly Pig would not
keep still. Soon everybody in the
theater was moaning and groan-
ing, "Keep still, Wriggly Pig!"

The Pigs had no choice but to
get up and go.

The Pigs decided to go to the beach instead. Soon Mr. and Mrs. Pig were drifting off to sleep in the warm, peaceful sun.

But Wriggly Pig could not see the point of sleeping in the middle of the day. He tossed and turned and sent showers of sand all over the place.

"Keep still, Wriggly Pig!" said Bradley. "You're getting sand in the lunch box."

But Wriggly Pig would not keep still. There was sand in the sandwiches, sand in the lemonade, and sand in Mr. Pig's ear.

"That's it!" said Mr. Pig. "We'll go somewhere where there's no sand."

Next, the Pigs went to play miniature golf. They lined up with their putters at the first hole. It was Brenda's turn first. Mrs. Pig said "Ssh!" Mr. Pig and Bradley were as quiet as mice. But Wriggly Pig was not quiet at all. Wriggly Pig hummed and whistled and swung with his putter.

"Keep still, Wriggly Pig!" said Brenda. "You'll throw me off!"

But Wriggly Pig would not keep still. He made Brenda so nervous she hit her ball right over the wall. There was a loud SMASH!

"That's your fault, Wriggly Pig!" said Brenda, and the Pigs ran as fast as they could back to the car.

The Pigs were getting very fed up. They decided to go to a café.

It was a polite kind of café, where everyone spoke softly and sat quietly. Everyone, that is, except for Wriggly Pig. He played with the menu and tugged at the tablecloth and kept scratching under his arm.

"Keep still, Wriggly Pig!" said Mrs. Pig. "Everyone will think we've got fleas!"

The sheep at the next table heard Mrs. Pig say *fleas*. They looked at Wriggly Pig, they looked at each other, then they got up and left.

Soon there was no one in the café but the Pigs. "That's the last straw, Wriggly Pig!" said Mrs. Pig. "We're taking you to see a doctor!"

Wriggly Pig did not like the doctor's office. He quivered and trembled and wriggled more than usual.

"Hmm," said the doctor. "It sounds like Wriggle Fever or maybe Fidget-itis. I shall have to examine this pig."

Wriggly Pig did not want to be
examined.

"Keep still, Wriggly Pig!" said
the doctor, and he pressed his cold,
cold hoofs on Wriggly's belly.

That was enough for Wriggly
Pig. He leapt off the table, dived
through the doctor's legs and
vanished through the door.

Wriggly Pig had never run so fast in his life. He raced down the stairs,

through the waiting room,

and out into the street.

He ran down the sidewalk with his feet flying,

dashed around the corner...and went BANG! straight into
a mailbox.

Wriggly Pig lay very still.

"Are you all right, Wriggly Pig?" asked Mrs. Pig. Wriggly Pig did not answer.

"Wake up, Wriggly Pig!" said Mr. Pig.

Wriggly did not move a muscle.

Mr. and Mrs. Pig and Brenda and Bradley began to get very upset.

Then Wriggly's ear twitched.

His snout gave a sniff.

His tail gave a wriggle

and his eyes opened.

Soon Wriggly Pig was wriggling all over. He wriggled more than the wriggliest worm and the squirmiest snake.

The Pigs breathed a sigh of relief. They hugged Wriggly, then they hugged each other.

"From now on," said Wriggly Pig, "I am going to try to keep still."

"No!" said the other Pigs. "Keep wriggling, Wriggly Pig!" And the whole family wriggled all the way home.

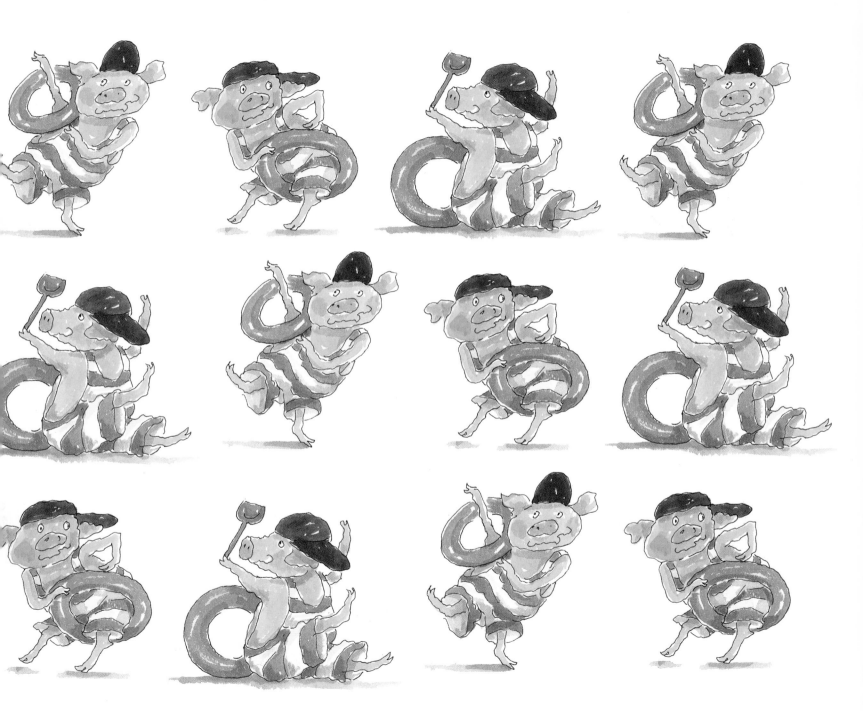